Betsey
Biggalow
is Here!

Betsey
Biggalow
is Here!

Malorie Blackman

Illustrated by
Lis Toft

mammoth

To Neil
With Love

First published in Great Britain 1992
by Piccadilly Press Ltd
Published 1993 by Mammoth
Reissued 1998 by Mammoth
an imprint of Egmont Children's Books Ltd
239 Kensington High Street, London W8 6SA

ISBN 0 7497 1421 2

10 9 8 7 6 5 4 3 2

A CIP catalogue record for this title
is available from the British Library

Printed and bound in Great Britain
by Cox & Wyman Ltd, Reading, Berkshire

CONTENTS

The Special, Special Trainers!

Betsey peered in through the shoe shop window. There they were! Her special trainers. Her magic trainers. With those trainers she wouldn't just run, she'd *fly*! No one would be able to catch her in those extra special, *special* trainers.

'Betsey, come away from that window.' Gran'ma Liz frowned.

'Oh Gran'ma Liz. Look! The trainers I was telling you about – they're still there!' Betsey pointed.

'They're going to stay there too!' Gran'ma Liz said. 'Come on.'

'But I need a new pair of trainers,' said Betsey. 'Mine are worn to nothing now.'

'I don't know how you can get through the soles of your shoes so fast.' Gran'ma Liz tutted. 'You must be eating them!'

'Gran'ma Liz, just look at these trainers. Look at the colours. Look at the laces. Look at the . . .'

'Look at the time!' Gran'ma Liz glanced down at her watch. 'Come on Betsey, or we'll miss our bus.'

'But Gran'ma Liz . . .'

'Betsey, for the last time, I'm not buying you those trainers. For weeks now all your mam and I have heard from you is trainers this and trainers that!'

'But Gran'ma Liz, my best friend

May has a pair of those trainers,'
Betsey said eagerly, 'and you should see
her when she runs. She doesn't run, she
soars and swoops – just like a bird or a
plane.'

'Betsey, you talk some real nonsense
sometimes,' said Gran'ma Liz. 'Come
on, child.'

So Betsey had to leave the front of
the shoe shop. She crossed her fingers
tight, tight, tight.

'I want those trainers something
fierce,' Betsey muttered to herself.

'What did you say, Betsey?' asked
Gran'ma Liz.

'Nothing, Gran'ma,' said Betsey.

'Hhmm!' said Gran'ma. 'Hhmm!'
And without another word, off they
went home.

But on the way home, Betsey had an
idea . . .

At dinner time, the family sat around

the table. Gran'ma Liz and Betsey and
Sherena, Betsey's bigger sister and
Desmond, Betsey's bigger brother. For
dinner there was cou-cou and flying
fish and salad and a huge jug of
delicious soursop drink mixed with
milk and plenty of ice. Betsey licked her
lips. Scrumptious!

'Pass the salt please, Betsey,' said Sherena.

Betsey picked up the glass salt shaker. 'The tops of the trainers I want are just as white as this salt,' said Betsey.

She pointed to the pepper bottle.

'And the soles of the trainers I want are blacker than the writing on the pepper bottle.' Sherena and Desmond looked at each other.

'Betsey, I want to hear no more about those trainers. D'you hear?' frowned Gran'ma Liz.

'Yes, Gran'ma,' Betsey said.

Betsey poured herself a glass of soursop drink, but some spilt onto the sky-blue tablecloth. The white liquid spread out.

'Betsey!' said Gran'ma Liz. 'Look at that mess.'

'That stain is just about the size of

the trainers I want,' Betsey murmured.

Gran'ma Liz could stand it no longer.

'Elizabeth Ruby Biggalow, all day, all week, all *month*, you've done nothing but mope and whine about those trainers,' frowned Gran'ma Liz. 'Your long face is spoiling my day as well as my dinner. Now not another word.'

And Betsey knew then that she'd better shut up. Whenever Gran'ma Liz called her by her whole, full name, Betsey knew she was treading dangerously close to trouble.

But for the rest of the evening all Betsey had in her head were her special trainers. She even fell asleep dreaming of soaring and flying, her special trainers on her feet.

The next morning, when Betsey went down for breakfast, everyone was unusually quiet.

'What's the matter?' asked Betsey.

'I've got something for you.' Mam smiled. 'As your old trainers are in such a state I decided to get you some new ones.'

'You bought the trainers!' Betsey couldn't believe it.

'Now perhaps we can all get some peace,' Gran'ma Liz sniffed.

Betsey grinned and grinned. Her extra special trainers. She'd got them at last. Mam handed over the bag she was

hiding behind her back. Betsey opened
the bag and . . .

'What's the matter?' asked Sherena.

'Oh!' Betsey couldn't say anything
else. Her eyes started stinging and there

was a huge, choking lump in her
throat. Botheration! These weren't the
trainers she wanted. Where were the
ones with the white fronts and the
black soles and the red laces? Where

were her special trainers? Still in the shop – that's where!

These ones were pink and grey and didn't have any black writing on them like the ones she wanted.

'Betsey . . .' Gran'ma Liz warned. 'Your mam had to take time off work to buy those for you.'

'Don't you like them, Betsey?' Mam asked.

'They're lovely,' Betsey whispered.

'Put them on then,' urged Desmond.

Betsey sat down and, oh so slowly she put on her new shoes.

'They look boss!' smiled Sherena.

'The best trainers I've ever seen,' said Desmond.

Gran'ma Liz didn't say anything. She just watched Betsey.

'Can I go and show them to my friend May please?' Betsey asked Mam.

'Go ahead then,' she smiled. 'But

don't stay with her too long. You've still got your morning chores to finish.'

Betsey ran out of the kitchen. She couldn't wait to get out of the house. She looked down at her feet. These shoes weren't her special trainers. These shoes were just horrible. Betsey ran all the way to May's house - sprinting as if to sprint the trainers right off her feet. At May's house, Betsey knocked and knocked again. May opened the door. Worse still, May opened the door wearing the very same trainers that Betsey wanted so much.

'Hi May,' Betsey said glumly.

'Hi Betsey,' said May. 'I was just going to the beach. Coming?'

Betsey shrugged. 'Just for a little while.'

So off they went. But things weren't right. No, they weren't. By the time Betsey and May reached the beach they were having a full blown, full grown argument.

'Well, my trainers are the best in the country,' said May.

'My trainers are the best in the world,' Betsey fumed.

'Talk sense! My trainers are the best in the universe,' said May.

'I hate you and your trainers,' Betsey shouted. 'And I hate these ones I'm wearing and I hate *everything*.'

'And I hate you and your smelly shoes too,' May stormed.

Betsey and May stared and glared and scowled and glowered at each other.

Then Betsey started to smile, then to laugh, then to hold her stomach she was laughing so much.

'What's so funny?' May asked, still annoyed.

'Botheration! Imagine hating a pair of shoes!' Betsey laughed. 'You hate my

11

shoes and I hate your shoes. And both pairs of shoes are probably laughing at us for being so foolish.'

'All this fuss over a pair of trainers,' May agreed with a giggle.

'Come on! Let's have a run. Things are always better after a run on the beach,' said Betsey. 'I'll race you to that palm tree yonder.'

'Ready . . . Set . . . Go . . .'

And off they both sprinted, faster than fast. They leapt over the sand and through the lapping water, kicking up the spray as they went, laughing and laughing. Until finally they both collapsed in the shade of the palm tree Betsey had pointed to. Who won the race? Neither May nor Betsey cared.

Betsey glanced down at her wet shoes. They were all right! Not the ones she'd wanted, but a present from her mam just the same. A special present.

A wonderful surprise.

'Look at that!' said May, surprised. May pointed to her trainers. The red colour in her laces was running down the white front of her trainers and over the black writing. May's trainers didn't like getting wet – not one little bit.

Betsey glanced down at her own trainers – still grey and pink and no running colours anywhere. She jumped up.

'May, let's walk along the beach for a bit longer,' said Betsey. 'We can collect shells and paddle. Never mind our trainers. Let's walk along in our bare feet.'

'Yeah! It's much nicer walking on the sand in bare feet anyway,' May agreed.

And May and Betsey ran over the white sand and through the blue water, their trainers knotted at the laces and dangling around their necks.

Betsey Biggalow Is Here!

Betsey Biggalow had another of her bright and shiny ideas! Today would be her HELP THE WORLD day! The question was, who should she help first? She ran into the sitting-room. Sherena was sitting at the table, books, books and more books spread out in front of her.

'Have no fear! Betsey Biggalow is here!' said Betsey proudly.

'Not now, Betsey. Can't you see I'm busy?' said Sherena.

Betsey walked across to peer over her sister's shoulder.

'What're you doing?'

Sherena looked up, annoyed. 'I'm trying, *trying* to revise for my Maths test on Monday.'

'I'll help you,' Betsey insisted.

'You can help me by disappearing,' Sherena said crossly. 'Go on! Vanish! Depart! Leave! Go away!'

'All right. You don't have to go on,' said Betsey. 'If you don't need my help, I'll go and find someone who does.'

'You do that!' said Sherena, her head buried back in the book in front of her.

Betsey ran out into the backyard to see her brother. Desmond was feeding the fowls which clucked and pecked and pecked and clucked.

'Have no fear! Betsey Biggalow is here!' said Betsey. 'I've come to help.'

'I don't need the help of a shrimp like

you,' Desmond scoffed. 'Besides, how come you wait till I've almost finished, before coming to help me?'

'Well, I'm here now,' said Betsey. Helping the world was turning out to be more difficult than she'd ever imagined.

'Betsey Biggalow, what are you up to?' Gran'ma Liz came out into the yard. 'If you're seeking useful employment, I can soon find a hundred and one things for you to do.'

Betsey shuddered. She was looking for one interesting something to do — not a hundred and one boring somethings!

'No thanks, Gran'ma Liz,' said Betsey. 'I was just about to go and see my friend May.'

'Hhmm!' said Gran'ma Liz. 'Well, just make sure you're back before supper.'

Betsey didn't need to be told twice. It was time to scarper before Gran'ma Liz decided that her one hundred and one things should come before a visit to May.

So off Betsey went, down the track, along the road, to May's house. The evening sun was still hot, hot, hot and the sugar cane in the fields on either side of the road, cast long, evening shadows.

'Botheration! So much for "Have no fear, Betsey Biggalow is here!"' Betsey muttered with disgust.

And so much for helping the world. You just couldn't help the world when it didn't want your help. Betsey was so deep in thought that she almost didn't hear it. She stopped, and frowned and looked around. Then it came again.

'Help . . . oh please help me . . .'

Frightened, Betsey looked around. 'Who's that? Who's there?'

'Over here . . .' the faint voice said.

Slowly, oh so slowly and oh so carefully, Betsey crept over towards the voice. Then she saw him. There, lying in a ditch by the side of the road, was a man with a moustache. He was lying half on his side, half on his back. And there, on top of his left leg, was a motorbike.

'I . . . I think I've broken my leg,' the man whispered. Betsey could see the perspiration all over his cheeks and his chin. His wet face glistened in the evening sunshine. His shirt was damp and sticking to him just as closely as Gran'ma Liz's Sunday hat stuck to her head.

'Wait . . . wait there. I'll go and get my gran'ma,' Betsey said. 'I'll be right back.'

'What's your . . . your name . . .'
asked the man.

'Betsey. Betsey Biggalow.'

'Hurry Betsey . . .' the man gasped,
before his eyes closed and his head
nodded down towards the ground.

Betsey ran. She raced like the wind.

'Gran'ma Liz! Gran'ma Liz! There's

a man. And he's broken his leg. And he's lying in a ditch. And his motorbike is lying on his leg. And his eyes are closed. And . . .'

'Calm down, child,' frowned Gran'ma Liz. 'Now what're you saying?'

So Betsey explained all over again. The words fell over each other, each one in a rush to be heard. Desmond came in from the garden and Sherena left her books in the sitting-room to listen. By the time Betsey had finished explaining she was out of breath.

'You'd better take us to him,' Gran'ma Liz said. Gran'ma Liz got a blanket and off they all went. At last they reached the part of the road where Betsey had seen the man and his motorbike in the ditch. And he was still there, his eyes closed, his body as still as Sunday morning.

'Sherena, run back to the house and phone for an ambulance. Desmond, Betsey, help me move this motorbike off his leg.' Gran'ma Liz got busy at once.

'Is he all right?' Desmond puffed as they tried to shift the motorbike.

'He's still breathing and that's something,' said Gran'ma Liz. 'He's unconscious. The pain was probably too much.'

'Should we move him?' asked Betsey.

'No. When someone's been in a road accident you shouldn't move them. The ambulance men will know how to move him the right way,' Gran'ma Liz said. 'I'll cover him with this blanket I brought with me.'

'Why does he need a blanket? It's hot-baking!' said Betsey.

'Anyone who's had a shock should be kept warm. You can get cold very quickly when you've had a serious accident. We'll stand and watch over him until the ambulance arrives.'

'Look, Gran'ma Liz. The front tyre of his bike is flat.' Desmond pointed. 'He must have got a puncture and skidded off the road.'

'If the good Lord had meant for us to go tearing around to up, down, below and above, we would have petrol in our bodies, not blood,' Gran'ma Liz sniffed. Gran'ma Liz didn't approve of cars and motorbikes.

After a long, short time, the ambulance finally arrived, its lights flashing, its siren wailing. Betsey watched, holding her breath, as the ambulance men lifted the man with the broken leg onto a stretcher. The injured man's eyes fluttered open and saw Betsey.

'It's okay. You're going to the

hospital now,' said Betsey.

'Thank you, Betsey,' smiled the man.
'I'm going to be fine now.' And he
closed his eyes as he was carried over to
the ambulance. In only a few moments,
the ambulance went roaring away
towards the hospital, its siren wailing.

'Will the man and his leg be all right?' asked Betsey.

'He'll be fine. At the hospital they'll fix him up in no time,' smiled Gran'ma Liz. 'Betsey, you did very well. You were right to come and get me.'

Betsey thought hard for a moment.

'I didn't help the whole world today,' she said. 'But I did help a little bit of it. I think that's okay.'

'Of course it's okay. I'm proud of you, Betsey,' said Gran'ma Liz.

And what did Betsey do? Betsey just smiled.

Betsey and the Mighty Marble

'I've got a marble. A mighty marble,' said Josh proudly. School had finished for the day and there was still plenty of afternoon left to play in. Betsey and her friends were on the beach.

'Who wants to look at my mighty marble?' Josh called out.

'Me! Me!' Everyone shouted.

Josh held out his marble in the palm of his hand. Betsey's brown eyes sparkled brighter than sunshine on the clear blue sea behind her. Ooooh! All eyes were on Josh's marble. Oh, how it glittered! Oh, how it glistened! Betsey had never seen anything like it.

'I told you,' said Josh. 'Isn't it terrific?'

It was the biggest marble Betsey had ever seen and it was filled with sky blue and leaf green and moonlight silver slivers.

'It's the most beautiful marble in the world,' Betsey breathed. And all at once, she wanted that marble. She wanted that marble something fierce.

'Josh,' began Betsey, holding up her bag of marbles. 'I'll swap you ten of my best marbles for your mighty marble.'

'No way,' Josh scoffed. 'Mr Mighty Marble is staying with me!'

'I'll swap you *twenty* of my marbles for your mighty marble,' said May.

Soon the air was filled with 'I'll swap you this', and 'I'll swap you that', but

Josh only laughed and held Mr Mighty
Marble up higher.

Betsey looked at the super marble in
Josh's hands. It seemed to be calling
out to her, teasing her.

'Betsey . . .' whispered Mr Mighty
Marble. 'Betsey, look at me. Aren't I
just the most perfect, the most splendid
marble in the world!' And what could
Betsey reply but, 'You are! You are!'

Betsey dug her hand into her dress
pocket and slowly took out Old

Faithful. Old Faithful was a small marble, perfect and clear, with a single gold streak like a summer lightning flash caught in its middle. Betsey's dad had given it to her.

'You look after Old Faithful,' said Dad. 'And Old Faithful will look after you.'

It was Betsey's special marble and all her friends admired it, but Betsey never played with it. Old Faithful was too small to play with.

'Josh,' said Betsey. 'let's have a contest, right now. Your Mr Mighty Marble against my best marble.'

'Why should I?' frowned Josh.

''Cause if you win, I'll give you every marble I've got,' said Betsey slowly. She held up her full bag of marbles. 'You'll get every single marble in here.'

Josh's eyes gleamed. 'Including Old Faithful?'

Betsey looked at the marble her dad had given her. Next to Mr Mighty Marble, Old Faithful looked dull and titchy-tiny and hardly worth bothering with at all.

'Including Old Faithful,' Betsey agreed at last.

'Betsey! You can't do that,' said May. 'Your dad gave you Old Faithful.'

'May, don't you worry,' said Betsey. 'If I win, I'll get Josh's super marble.'

'And what happens if you lose?' asked May, her hands on her hips.

Betsey thought about it, long and hard. If she lost then Josh would end up with every single marble she had in the world – including Old Faithful. Dad had played marbles with Old Faithful when he was a boy and he'd given her Old Faithful as a present. How could she give away a present from her dad?

She shouldn't have told Josh she'd give him Old Faithful. What if she *did* lose and Dad found out?

'Josh, I think . . .' Betsey began.

'You're not changing your mind, are you? You're not turning chicken?' Josh called out. 'Cluck! Clu-uu-ck! Chicken!'

'No, I'm not. I'm ready when you are,' said Betsey. But as she spoke she was careful not to look at May. That didn't mean that she couldn't hear May tutting beside her though.

Josh walked to his starting position which was at the end of the path that led to the beach. Everyone followed him. May pulled Betsey back from the crowd.

'Betsey, you're making a big mistake.' May shook her head.

'Botheration, May! You're not my gran'ma. Don't you try to boss my head,' said Betsey, annoyed.

'Are you really going to let Josh take all your marbles?' asked May. 'Even the one your dad gave you?'

'I'm going to win Josh's mighty marble,' Betsey said stubbornly. 'So Josh won't get any of my marbles. I won't lose a single one of them.'

'You've lost your marbles already if you think your itsy-bitsy bit of glass stands a chance against Josh's mighty marble,' said May.

Betsey began to feel bad. Worse than bad. Betsey began to feel terrible. She wished she'd never challenged Josh to this stupid contest.

'Come on then, Betsey,' Josh called out. 'I'm busting to win a whole bag of marbles.'

Betsey and May walked over to join Josh and the others.

'Josh, we can still have our contest but I don't want to include Old Faithful in it. My dad gave me Old Faithful and . . .'

But Josh didn't let Betsey finish.

'Cluck! Clu-uu-ck! Chicken!' Josh began to leap about and to peck and flap and strut, just like a chicken. 'Cluck! Clu-uu-ck!' Soon everyone else was doing the same thing. 'Clu-uu-ck!'

'Botheration!' said Betsey. 'Josh,

you're about to lose Mr Mighty Marble.'

Betsey dug into her bag.

'What are you doing?' Josh frowned.

'Getting out a marble to play with,' answered Betsey.

'You've got to use Old Faithful,' Josh said. 'That was the deal.'

'But that's not fair. Your mighty marble is ginormous and Old Faithful is tiddly,' said Betsey.

'Too bad. That's the deal,' smiled Josh.

What could Betsey do? The contest was all her idea so she couldn't back out now. There was nothing left to do but to stay put and play. Betsey felt her eyes stinging but she forced herself not to cry. She was going to lose all her precious marbles. All the marbles it had taken her so long to collect. And worse still, she was going to lose Old Faithful.

'Josh, you go first,' sniffed Betsey.

And the contest began. Everyone gathered round to watch. Josh flicked Mr Mighty Marble first. Betsey flicked Old Faithful away from Mr Mighty Marble. Josh flicked his marble towards Betsey's.

'Ooooh!' A gasp came from everyone around. Josh had only just missed Betsey's marble.

This was it. If Betsey didn't do something, Josh would hit her marble with his very next shot and then Betsey would lose every single marble she had in the world.

'Bombsies!' Betsey said.

Josh laughed. 'Bombsies! With that little marble! You can't win, Betsey, so give up now.'

'I'll show you,' Betsey said. She stood up, Old Faithful in her hand. She stood over Josh's marble carefully lining up

Old Faithful over Mr Mighty Marble.
If she missed, Josh would win for sure.
No one spoke. The only sound came
from the waves lapping on the white
sand and the sound of birds singing
from the trees.

'Your hand can't be lower than your waist,' Josh said.

'I know.' Betsey didn't look up. She carried on lining up her shot until Old Faithful was directly above Mr Mighty Marble. Then Betsey let go of her own marble. Old Faithful hit Mr Mighty Marble with a CRR-AAA–CK!

Then a strange thing happened. Old Faithful bounced off Mr Mighty Marble.

'Ooooh!' said everyone.

Josh's marble wasn't well. It wasn't well at all. Mr Mighty Marble, Mr Super Marble, Mr Bigger-than-anyone-else's Marble had cracked into four pieces. Each piece lay on the path, glistening and glittering just as loudly as before.

Betsey picked up Old Faithful and stared at it.

'Wow, Betsey. That's some marble,'

everyone said.

Josh carefully picked up the pieces that made up what used to be Mr Mighty Marble.

'Look what you did.' Josh stared down at the pieces in his hand.

'Mr Mighty Marble doesn't look so mighty any more,' May laughed.

'Sorry, Josh,' Betsey said. 'You can have any five of my marbles if you want.' Betsey held out her bag of marbles.

'Can I have Old Faithful?' Josh asked hopefully.

'No chance!' said Betsey firmly. 'Old Faithful may be small, but he's a real super marble.'

Josh looked down and kicked at the ground with the toe of his right shoe.

'Come on, Josh,' smiled Betsey. 'I'll give you my second best marble instead.'

'Oh, all right then,' Josh said at last. Betsey handed over her bag and let Josh pick out five marbles he wanted.

Then Betsey, May and all their friends set off for home, telling tales of Old Faithful, the mightiest marble of them all.

Betsey's Bad Day!

The moment Betsey opened her eyes,
she was awake. She grinned and sat up.
Saturday morning! And only one more
week until Dad came home. And no
school! *And* they were all going into
town today. Today was going to be a
good day!

'Yippee! Saturday!' Betsey sprang
out of bed.

She put on her slippers and went to
have her wash. When she'd finished,

she went for her breakfast. Sherena and Desmond were already at the table. So was Gran'ma Liz.

'Sit down, Betsey,' said Mam. 'I'll get your breakfast.' Betsey turned in her chair to look at Mam.

'What's for breakfast, Mam?' Betsey sniffed the air. 'Ham?'

'And scrambled eggs,' said Mam.

'Scrumptious,' grinned Betsey. She turned around. There before her was a long, cool glass of orange juice.

'Yumptious-scrumptious!' said Betsey. And she picked up the glass and started to drink. Oh, it was cold! Oh, it was refreshing! Oh, it was delicious!

'Betsey, you toad! That's *my* orange juice,' said Desmond.

'Then what's it doing in front of my plate?' Betsey replied.

'I don't know and I don't care,' said Desmond. 'It's still my orange juice.'

'Desmond boy, don't call your sister a toad,' said Gran'ma Liz. 'If she's a toad, then you must be one too 'cause you're her brother.' Desmond started to sulk.

'Desmond, there's plenty of orange juice for everyone, so behave,' said Mam. 'And Betsey, if you want some orange juice, pour some for yourself. Don't just help yourself to your brother's.'

'But . . . but . . .' Betsey protested. Botheration! The glass *had* been in front of her plate. Never mind, today was *Saturday*! Betsey handed over her now half empty glass to Desmond.

'Huh!' said Demond, still sulking. He put the glass to his lips and finished his orange juice with one gulp. Then he poured himself another one.

'Pass the sugar, Betsey,' said Sherena, stirring her coffee.

43

'Manners!' said Gran'ma Liz. 'What do you say?'

'Please,' said Sherena. 'Please, please, please!'

With a grin, Betsey handed over the sugar bowl. Sherena added a spoonful of sugar to her coffee, then another spoonful, then another, and another.

'Sherena girl, by the time you're sixteen, you'll not have one tooth left in

your head if you carry on like that,'
said Gran'ma Liz.

'I like it sweet, Gran'ma Liz,' smiled
Sherena. 'Besides, I want to put on
weight. I'm as skinny as a needle –
worse luck. Everyone says so.' Sherena
lifted her coffee cup to her lips. She'd
barely taken one sip when immediately
she started to gag and cough. The cup
fell from her hand. Both hands flew to

her throat, as she coughed and spluttered and coughed some more, her eyes watering.

'Sherena? Sherena, what's the matter?' Mam ran over to her and so did Gran'ma Liz. Betsey sprang out of her chair. 'Sherena, are you all right?'

'Salt!' Sherena coughed. 'There's s-salt in that bowl, not s-sugar.'

'Whose turn was it to fill the sugar bowl last night?' Mam frowned. All eyes turned slowly to Betsey. Betsey's mouth dropped open.

'I thought I put sugar in it – honest!' she said quickly. Mam took the sugar bag and the salt bag out of the cupboard.

'Which bag did you use?' she asked.

Betsey stared at the bags. One was white and red, the other was red all over. The first bag said SALT on it and the second bag said FINEST SUGAR.

'Er . . . I . . . er . . .' began Betsey.

'I'm waiting, Betsey.' Mam pursed her lips.

'I used the white and red bag to fill the sugar bowl,' Betsey admitted, adding quickly. 'But it wasn't my fault. The salt bag was on the kitchen table and I thought it was the sugar bag and I was in a hurry because I was missing the film on the T.V . . .'

'More haste, less speed.' Gran'ma Liz wagged her finger.

Mam frowned. 'Betsey! What is the matter with you today? First you drink your brother's orange juice, then you try to poison your sister.'

'But it wasn't purpose work,' said Betsey. 'It wasn't deliberate. I only . . .'

'Betsey, if you carry on like this, we'll leave you with May's parents and go to town without you,' said Mam. 'If I take you into town, goodness only knows what havoc you'll cause.'

'I won't cause any havoc, Mam. I promise,' Betsey said quickly. She didn't want to miss the trip into town. No, she didn't!

'So you say,' said Mam. 'But you've only been awake for two seconds and look what's happened already.'

Betsey couldn't argue with that so she said nothing. She thought a lot though. And her thoughts started with 'botheration' and ended with 'botheration'!

At least it's Saturday – and only seven more days till Dad comes home, Betsey thought to herself. That thought cheered her up a little.

After breakfast, they all had to hurry up and get ready in order to catch the bus into town. In her bedroom, Betsey kicked off her slippers and looked around for the pink and grey trainers her mam had bought her. She found

one by the bedroom door where she
and Sherena always left their shoes but
could she find the other one? No, she
couldn't! Betsey searched high and low,
under the bed and in the bottom of the
wardrobe.

'Betsey! Speed up!' Mam called out.
'Coming, Mam,' Betsey called back.
Betsey hunted to the left of the
bedroom and to the right of the

bedroom and she still couldn't find her other trainer.

'BETSEY!' Mam said. 'What are you doing? We're going to miss our bus.'

'Mam, I can't find one of my trainers,' Betsey yelled.

'Then wear your sandals, but hurry up! That bus won't wait forever.'

Betsey stood in the middle of the room, her hands on her hips. Botheration! Double botheration! Where *was* that other trainer?

'Betsey!' Mam came into the room. 'Come on.'

'But Mam, I wanted to wear my trainers,' Betsey said.

Mam looked around the room. She pointed to under the bureau. 'Isn't that your other shoe?'

Betsey looked down. There, just sticking out from the bottom of the chest of drawers was the other trainer.

'But Mam, I didn't put my trainer there . . .' Betsey said, puzzled.

'It didn't crawl under there by itself, Betsey. What has got into you this morning?' Mam sighed. 'Now, put on your trainer and let's go.'

At last they left the house. Demond walked with Gran'ma Liz and Sherena walked with Mam. Betsey walked by herself behind everyone else. They were all talking and laughing. Everyone except Betsey.

'I might as well call today My-Bad-Day instead of Saturday,' Betsey muttered to herself. 'Seems like everything I touch is going wrong and nothing I do is going right.'

Betsey sighed and sighed some more. Gran'ma Liz turned around.

'Betsey, we're off to town,' smiled Gran'ma Liz. 'So put your face straight before the wind changes direction and your face is stuck with that gloomy look on it. We'll get our provisions and when we've finished we can all go for an ice-cream.'

Ice-cream! Scrumptious! Double scrumptious! That was more like it!

The bus came along and juddered to a halt just as they all reached the bus stop.

'Jump up! Jump up!' laughed Gran'ma Liz. 'We're off to town!'

And they all scrambled aboard. Soon

they'd reached the market in town.

The town was even busier and better than Betsey remembered. They didn't come to town too often as there were plenty of small shops locally. But about once a month, they all climbed aboard a bus and went shopping for the provisions they couldn't buy from the local shops. Betsey sniffed the air. She could smell plantain cooking and fried fish and all different kinds of fruit like freshly picked bananas and mangoes and paw-paws and coconuts. Yumptious-scrumptious!

Betsey grinned. Saturday felt better already. Then Betsey saw something that made her eyes open wide as plates and made her mouth drop open and made her heart beat faster than fast. There, across the street. Dad!

'Dad! DAD!' Betsey yelled out.

Dad heard Betsey's voice and turned.

He grinned and waved and once the
road was clear, ran across it. Dad!
There followed such huggings and
cuddlings.

'I wasn't expecting you for another
week.' Mam smiled happily.

'My last exam wasn't meant to be
until the end of next week but they

brought it forward so I've finished all my exams now.' Dad grinned. 'I decided not to tell you all but to surprise you. My plane landed about an hour ago.'

'Are you a doctor yet?' Betsey asked eagerly.

'Not yet, Betsey.' Dad shook his head. 'I've got one more year of studying to do first.'

'So how long are you going to be home for?' asked Gran'ma Liz.

'A few weeks.' Dad grinned. 'The exams are over and I'm on holiday.'

'Yippee!' Sherena and Desmond shouted.

'I knew it.' Betsey smiled. 'I knew today was going to be a good day!'

And she was right!

Malorie Blackman

BETSEY BIGGALOW THE DETECTIVE

What can have happened to Betsey's teddy bear? She's disappeared without trace and there's only one clue. Betsey the Detective comes on the scene and, with the help of Prince, the detective dog, makes a very surprising discovery.

Betsey also puts on a show for the rest of the family, tries to ride Sherena's bicycle and almost flies a kite in this second book of stories, set on the Caribbean.

The sequel to *Betsey Biggalow is Here!*

Malorie Blackman

HURRICANE BETSEY

When Betsey hears that a hurricane is approaching the island she's very excited – she wants to spin up in the air – and is disappointed when she finds out that she'll have to stay indoors. Bored with waiting, Betsey decides she's going to *be* a hurricane – and Hurricane Betsey causes far more damage than the real one!

In this third collection of stories set on a Caribbean island, Betsey annoys her brother and sister, enters an insult contest and has a monster hamburger.

Malorie Blackman

MAGIC BETSEY

'Ladies and gentlemen . . . Betsey the magnificent will now put on a magic show for you!'

But Betsey's show is far from magnificent and by the end of her performance, Sherena's cards are ruined and Desmond is soaked. Then, with the help of a surprise visitor, Betsey comes up with the most amazing trick . . .

This is the fourth collection of stories about Betsey and her adventures.